Conversations at Genesis

INNOCENT THOUGHTS ABOUT LOVE

PRATIKSHA MISHRA

INDIA • SINGAPORE • MALAYSIA

ISBN
Paperback 979-8-89724-997-8
Hardcase 979-8-89744-968-2

“No I cannot find another you of any kind as I am hell bound to find you inside me someday”

This book is dedicated to my late dad with whom conversations were a breeze and everyone just loved the way he made conversations nothing more than an emotionally uplifted sensation underneath.

Miss You Dad

Contents

Introducing Conversations at Genesis: Innocent Thoughts About Love

I remember those Sunday mornings from my childhood days, the days when I was still lazy to wake up, while I can hear my mom and dad, talking from the room next door, while the famous show "Rangoli" (a 90s show, where they used to play movie songs that were selected from the precious collection of Hindi classics) was playing on the TV. They spoke to each other about random things, their childhood, the actors in the movie, the parts of the movies they like and why. As I heard them chatter, for some reason, there is a peaceful rhythm that plays on my mind alongside the faint music of the song, as I try to hear the words and guess the movie.

I remember the times when I was very much in love and wanted every moment to be constantly with the one, I loved. So being in a distant relationship didn't really help much, but the phone calls, which were expensive at that time, when both of us had just started our first jobs, were the only times we spoke to each other that kept the warmth of our closeness intact, despite the distance.

I remember the times when my daughter came back from school, and looked out for me, to talk her heart out, about all the things that happened at school.

Conversations are emotional instigators; they are the ones who make or break your ways of living your life. This book is about some conversations, that even for an animal, are essential to keep it going, the little things that we speak to each other, the nothings that we approach each other for, just to be with each other, the flow of thoughts inside our minds always conversing with ourselves. What am I doing? Why did this happen? Where is this going?

I am releasing this in the eve of "Valentine's Day", to just make relationships easier to maintain and grow with conversations that matter the most. This book consists of poems, quotes, essays and 3+1 bonus love stories, never published before. Let's start bringing these innocent thoughts into our conversations, because the more we talk amongst ourselves and to our inner selves, the better we can

Acknowledgements

I thank my parents and elder brother, who always were my guiding light towards having meaningful conversations, some difficult ones, some mad ones, some glad ones but never lonely ones. I thank my best friend who is now my husband, despite not loving the art of talking more, when we started our friendship back in college days, still got to become the recipient of some great conversations for almost some 20 plus years now. I also thank my school friends, teachers, neighbors, relatives and the people I met and had some fascinating conversations with.

Conversations: When

When you come..
The next time around.
Look out for me.
When you ask..
In amidst the sound.
Hear me out.
When you follow..
The path you found.
Wait up for me.
When you do..
I will be there.
When you don't..
Never stop to care.
When you see..
Close out on me.
When you find..
Freeze your thoughts on me.

When you forget..
Pretend to know me.
When you regret..
Try to go polite on me.

When I am gone
Will you find me?
When I am gone
Will you still
Talk to me
When I am gone
Will your silences
Still look
To be filled in by me
When I am gone
Will you try to hear everything?
That I was trying to say
When I am gone
Will you still stick around?
As I want you to pick everything
That I wanted for the rest of the ride
To understand my side
So that when we meet again
We forget the part
When I was gone..

When she
Didn't come
Last night
I couldn't
Leave her
Out of sight

When she
Didn't respond
After a fight
I forgave her
Even though

I was right
When she kept
Holding me tight
I thought
She will never abandon me
But that's when she told me
She isn't going
To show up
Last night..

Conversations: Love Is When

Love is when
you sit
right beside
and not a word

Love is when
you walk
alongside
and hands touch

Love is when
you see a smile
and you feel
you can keep looking
at it for a while

Love is when
no one knows
but you still do something
for someone to know

Love is when
you think
but one is forced
not to do so

Love is when
they come closer
and you wipe your face
to kiss them safe

Love is when
you die
as they cry
on your lap

Love is when
you fight with nights
to get a sight
of the moon

Love is when
you try to blend
but it's too obvious
to undo pretend

Love is when
you are trapped
yet
feel free
to live for someone
that's not you

Conversations: Friendly Addiction

How often have you had the urge to shout out loud when you are sitting quietly among a crowd of people advised to be silent all the while with no movement what so ever.

How often have you had the urge to call someone who has repeatedly asked you not to..

How often have you had the urge to see someone when you very well know that person doesn't want to meet you or will never talk to you ever again..

How often have you had the urge to run away from a party where you are among the ones hosting the guests and in charge of making them feel comfortable..

How often have you had the urge to just start singing a song loud enough so that you ignore the preacher who wants you to follow the miracles of life which seems practically impossible...

How often have you had the urge to jump into a waterfall knowing very well that you would die as you don't know swimming very well..

How often have you had the urge to just say sorry and make things better when you know it's never going to unwind as before..

How often have you had the urge to actually smile instead of crying when someone close to you just dies.. to cherish their memories as you think about the times you spent with them and how suddenly now it will become worthy of it's existence in your life as a painful mark…

I know these have nothing related to addiction but somehow they all relate to the urge to do something when you very well know you are not supposed to that particular thing or doing so you are not going to make much of a difference but you still can't control the urge of going ahead and doing it.

"Because Your Eyes Said

You Were Feeling It Too"

There are certain relationships you get addicted to and even if you want to it's not easy enough to break free no matter how many times your brains talk you out of it.

Have always been addicted to friendships since childhood over all relationships. Sometimes I ended up fighting with family and loved ones due to friends.

While other times ended up alone as friends chose other priorities over friendship forcing me to read the obvious as they had completely moved on with me still waiting for them to come back to the very same spot they chose to quit.

As a kid was very shy on confronting someone and become friends effortlessly especially was fascinated by the word best friend which by now I think is just a fancy terminology with no actual intentions behind.

Since the beginning of time have been always been defined by a friend who has known to be closely associated with me.But as time went by started to realize more that it was my dependency not theirs which created these close associations.

Life has his own way of explaining things as we grow up.Sometimes it explains you in a detailed manner while most of the times they come in as a sudden jerk or a grave reality check.

For me there have been equal times of both experiences. There were times when my friend had chosen to go the other way because they wanted to refine their future and not to doom their ways with a notorious kid.This happened when I had just been shuffled away to a separate class from my closest circle of friends to help me get academically stronger as per the teachers way which resulted in one thing that the bond was definitely not strong enough as it got pulled by its roots pretty quickly.

There were times when I was called in for choices which I clearly hated as I believed friends are there to die for and not to take a pick at or make your best selection cause they just happen around the clock with absolute zero manipulation.

Towards high school they became lesser but the ones who stuck around were not less than a strong addiction of hanging together in thicks and thins. For some they pretended I didn't exist anymore as they moved to better colleges and there were incidents of me going to meet them and they either not turning up or lying on my face which I thought was absurdly annoying.

Those were probably the first times of being getting ignored so my heart was getting used to the ignoring phase which became quite popular afterwards.

At junior school being part of a popular girls group was a mandatory cult for a normal convent goer.But at that time being a shy person myself found it hard to please someone where all I wanted was to have fun or play in the limited recess time.I joined the junior kids instead who were pretty delighted to have me.Enjoyed their special treatment and funny innocence which gave me freedom to play without much thinking or gossiping around forcing someone to love me while getting admitted to their lives.

Things changed when I went off to college it all started with a lot of friends to a handful of friends followed by the day every single one of us parted to go in their own suitable direction.Not to mention things went way too complicated, life wasn't simple like the playtime anymore. It was when reality was kicking in every single second of our lives sometimes as a friend's broken heart, relationships based on lies, masked friends, fake world, money driving vultures,up and close with death of your dear one, annoying rules, peer pressure.

It becomes squishier while you keep experiencing good things and bad things in the form of regular packages. All the philosophy of righteousness, trust, love, devotion seems to be blurry as you keep encountering different tangents of the same right angle.

Sometimes in the form of you thinking you ended up with a wrong person or you trying too hard to be someone who the world accepts as perfect. Sometimes in the form of you being close to someone you just met a few seconds back and sometimes being absolutely clueless of what your partner is complaining about..

Alone as it comes to dwell in the real world …We all are into it many times not knowing that there is no one except you who needs to hold onto pulling yourself hard enough to get out through this pit of quicksand which we all elaborately name as hardships.

But even in the darkest of moments there is light somewhere down the other side of the tunnel. So for me they gave me strength to pull over the gruesome stunts fearlessly battling life's messiness with the filthiest jokes.

There won't be a lot in one's life but the one you have should be worth walking down the darkest streets telling him/her your darkest secrets without fearing any aftermath.

Conversations: Keep

I keep wondering if you were real,
Or you were just being nice to me..
I keep wondering if trust is two way,
Or it isn't an age old advice to me..
I keep wondering if love ever happened,
Or perhaps a rolling dice for me..
I keep wondering if failure is harder,
Or success lies to me..
I keep wondering if chastity is freedom,
Or honesty cries all over me..
I keep wondering if it's going to get better,
Or the stage has portrayed a psychic actor..
A pleading wish while fingers crossed,
Wept over the edge as coins got tossed..
A choice was inflicted,
As the results got me tricked..
Nobody shall realize except me,
And it is me who can flee..
Nevertheless if it's meant to be,

It's going to happen within a walking spree..
Cause I can't be forever true,
Without him not having the slightest clue.
Or among the very few,
Just keep wondering if only he knew..

Conversations: Heartbroken

"I cry for you,
I try for you,
I sometimes
lie for you,
but I want you
even though
you want
nothing else from me…"

Conversations: Maybe

Maybe she gets me,
Or maybe she doesn't,
Maybe she hates me,
Or maybe she doesn't,
Maybe my traits are subtle,
Or maybe they ought to be bold,
Maybe she will walk towards me,
Or maybe she won't,
Maybe she lives in my story forever
Or maybe her story didn't even lever,
But it seemed good to pretend to be her lover,
While imagining that there was something between us..

Conversations: Poet

I am a poet,
filled with riots,
while a pen holds onto me,
puts me on its chariot,
to fluster my thoughts,
urging them to…
scribble on a piece of paper,
that might not win the battle,
or stop the bloody slaughter,
but it will help calm down,
after-supper chatter.

Conversations: Music

"I waited
For the song to play
But she didn't stay
when the
song
did play
she had left
already
but I had
started to sing
intruding the
parody.."

Conversations: Sorrow

"There is
More
tomorrow
than sorrow
there is less
mess after
you figure
out the chapter
not to follow
right after.."

Conversations: Dogs

I love
Going out
I love doing
Nothing
Watching you
Drive
I love
Running after
Anything
That fly
I love
That life
is full of
Little Things
while everyone else is busy
attending
Big things

Conversations: Grasshopper

I am
A grasshopper
As it gets
Dark
You start
Hearing me clearer
I say one
Thing
But what you hear
Is my wing
I die
By getting
Squished
Mushed
Crushed
But I latch to green
Match with the unseen
Patch to
Be keen

All night long
Don't get me wrong
I don't trust the mean
Lurking around
In boxes..

Conversations: Falling In Love

"I didn't realize what it was about falling in love, until one day I was in it. The only problem was getting out of it isn't what someone can deal with right away. As the more you want to forget, the more it starts haunting you, in a bittersweet manner, your naive emotions pleading you not to let it go. But the fact is, it's just your alter ego, that cannot take an untimely rejection and is asking you to keep up with the wreck less follow. That very thought is hollow, as deep down you know, things won't be sane, and even if you happen to go back again, the intrinsic pain remains forever."

Conversations: Falling In Love

"If you don't come
I will understand,
but if you chose not to come,
I will be mad…"

“If you choose me,
Don’t lose me…”

"When you need me to stay,
Better say.."

"I am in love
with what matters to you in
becoming you…"

Story: Speechless Moon

As I got interrupted by our office coffee machine's loud hissing noise, I suddenly realized was still working with my eyes wide open.... Checked the time was past 11, was awake to achieve some trigger in the graphical analysis for our Client ‹s online ad campaign, the report which constitutes more of assumption and less of consumption. Rubbing off the sleep from my eyes, was struggling to get back to my desk. The Smoking Hot coffee was the only attraction at this moment which was dragging me to my desk to dig my eyes into the reports.

While trying to concentrate, I overheard our sleepy Tinku Bhai

-our office caretaker talking to someone "arey aap hi ka office hai, saahab (The office is all yours master)...", this made me leave my desk again and go to our reception corner, wanting to collect data for my personal database which kind of gets fascinated by the unusual stuff rather than the usual one.. That's why these days some media channels believe in creating unusual news if they don't have one in store. Unusual news any day will attract an over enthusiast mob.

On my way, the over enthusiast me hungry for gossip just before reaching destination got so excited, that I started to run resulting the collision of myself with a human body.

I didn't even realize who it was until I confronted the body, with knit brows only to turn over and confront a calm gentleman smiling at me.

Hi Tiksha How are you doing?

(It was Daksh; he was an ex-employee and a good old friend of mine from the same company. It had been a while since we were in touch with each other anymore and yes to mention he was very much in love with his Dhanno, the nickname for the girl whom he dated and we used to tease him by calling him by this name; on a serious note the girl›s name was Henna.

P.S. she was not a friend of mine)

I am doing well, what about you?

Long time so why are you up and here so late? (After a pause I guessed that was lot of questions at one go)

Hey I never see you around, I do pass by regularly

Yeah, To meet Your Dhanno (I know I sounded rude)

He smiled and winked saying "I wish she was your friend then we could have met often….

No Ways!!!! (Yeah, that was me)

I came here as it's her (Dhanno) birthday today, and wanted to give her a little surprise by piling her desk with goodies..

WOW… I exclaimed. What an amazing thought.

.(Grumbling inside - why do all dumb girls get their hands on smarter guys)

Gee Thanks Tiksha …We had the cake cutting at 12 along with her family and some friends, and after that I just rushed to give her this little surprise, and Hola! !!! I meet my good old buddy after so long , who can also be sweet to me tonight and help her friend out , if she doesn't mind, and yes if she isn't busy..

I smiled …Okay Daksh ….Okay that's It …I will help you my friend.

So Where's the cake ?(grinning at him)

It was 1.30 now, and I was almost done with my reports, but still had to calculate the results and make the summarized feedback .But somehow helping Daksh was a much better idea, as I was already super bored gazing at my screen for 12 long hours.

Another hot coffee, and marched towards Dhanno's desk which was far away than mine, usually I like it that ways, but tonight I felt the urge that it would have been nicer if she was somewhere closer. It would have been easier for me to hop in hop off between my desk and hers. In the present scenario it was a proper stroll of 10 minutes from my desk to hers, which was painful.

Daksh has started on with cleaning up her desk for the goodies .Daksh to me was always a perfect gentleman who always kept his promises and who made an extra effort for any relationship he handles. But somehow when he chose Dhanno, I was a bit disappointed .The day he proposed to her, he had taken my advice, but I was just a few months old friend to Daksh, so I didn›t even utter a word against her, instead advised her to go for it .Anyways when it comes to heart, I feel your mind has its own way in deciding what›s good for you, better not mess with them as from my experience, if somebody has made up his mind to love an individual ,my advising him not to go in that direction doesn›t make any difference what so ever. People learn by their own mistakes when it comes to heart. On the other hand Dhanno was a typical girl, with all the nauseating habits and tantrums of a dumb girl. I and our group personally never liked her, it was just that she looked good, but if only her looks could somehow match her nature, it would have been brilliant.

You seem to sit far away from her?

I smiled

so how have you been all these years; it's been 3 years since we last met. How is life treating you?

And how are you treating your life?

I am good, 3 years ... I didn't even realize...Life is good, going on a faster pace. How's yours? When are you both planning to get together?

Well, I am planning end of this year, let's see what madam (Dhanno) has to say about it ...

She has her views and I respect her views a lot ...

So what about you? Have you given permission to anyone special yet? Or still waiting?

Naah...I am good, still haven't found a reason to get married or stick to someone for the sake of a relationship

...I am good. Can live and laugh with my friends and family forever...

You are still the same.Chal let›s get going ...

The night seemed to pass slowly ...we both were talking, making fun of each other, sipping coffee together, blabbering, shouting, teasing each other, reviving the old days when we used to go out for cutting chai (Tea) together, talking about everyone in the group and so on...

Suddenly his mobile hops up ...and he just puts it on speaker as we both were busy blowing up balloons for Dhanno's desk. "HI Baby, What you doing?, it's my birthday today "

I chuckled ...

Yup my dear ...was sleeping and dreaming about you my sweetheart.

I chuckled again...

"Is There somebody else with you? ?,I just wanted to talk to you about some stuff Baby"

I started to get up and leave ....just then he held my hands and pulled me back on my chair, and with his eyes asked me to sit down and carry on with whatever I was doing...

Suddenly I felt the warmth and closeness with his touch ...but I immediately tried to shift-delete every thought going on in my mind and started to get busy with the balloons. Just when I heard Dhanno saying...

"Baby, your gift wasn't that impressive, now that you are going to get married to me.Start giving some real gifts and stop giving me toys, you have to prove your worth in front of my family, only then they will be proud of my choice»

Listening to that I was like - Is she really that dumb???, what is she bragging about???

I could feel Daksh getting uncomfortable, with me listening to all his personal stuff...

Instead he smiled and said my dear its really late can we talk about this in the morning birthday girl...

Okay Baby but please do think about what I said, and do act as per required. Good Night Baby Love You.....

Love you too my dear, have a cozy sleep...

He looked at me ...She is a little psyched about her family not liking me, don't you worry my dear...she over reacts...

So you gift her an expensive piece and you get the love of her family right.... (I was intentionally being sarcastic to make him feel, that he is taking too much of shit from Dhanno Rani)

Chill Tik... (He used to call me by that name). You is getting it wrong my dear. Let's enjoy this night, don't get into the filthiness of the tragic reality called life.

It was then I realized, that Daksh was happily aware of what was going on, it was just that he just wanted to avoid any hasty decision from his side, or the fact that he loved Dhanno unconditionally...(I am still figuring it out)

Hey Tiksha …lets go and grab some cutting chai..Babu Bhaiya will be around, we can have some idli's (An Indian delicacy) too…then we can go on a quick bike ride and then come back and give her desk a final finishing touch…with red roses.

I had really started to admire Daksh at this moment, because there are a few bunch of people left of his kind. Who can leave all the worldly hassles and can just love unconditionally and can rather make love get bored and sick of them, but they won't ever try to break out of it.

So we headed for the famous Babu Bhaiya's cutting chai along with some garma garam (steaming hot) idli.

It was already 2.30, with each other time was gliding rapidly.

I was getting closer to him; I was getting to know the real Daksh.

We shared some secrets, family issues; he expressed his disappointment towards this ruthless world. It was a total new experience to talk out without feeling any pressure, of what the person listening infers about you.

When Daksh listened to my reasoning, it felt lighter talking it out with him and so was he.

After a year of dating, Your Dhanno changed Tik

I was shocked believe me.

But I can't just walk out now, I love her and she needs me, Tik.

I chose not to say a word then, (I could feel the pain in his eyes when he was explaining to me, I didn't want to upsurge his pain anymore)

Daksh, trust me it happens in every relationship, after a while the rosiness of the relation disappears leaving us to face the harshness of life. No relation stays forever, after a while it just becomes a restricted bond where you get strangulated in.

I don't completely believe that. I agree that you get bored after a point and your relation becomes stagnant, but at the same time you have someone always close to you, who will understand you and care for you even when you say nothing. I mean at this age you are never left alone, there are friends, family surrounding you, but at one point in life, you will be sitting all alone, sick and tired of living your life just when somebody will come and hug you tightly… (When Daksh said these words, he had hugged me tightly in his arms)

"No matter what I will never let you go and will love you till the last breathe of my life …"

I had started to feel the warmth of his hug and was really ready to die in his arms that very moment. Just then I realized that it was Daksh's style of making me believe in Love as I was sure he still loved his Dhanno a lot…

Don't make me get used to it Daksh, you are already Dhanno's property. I tried hard to smile this time as smiling at that very moment was getting painful for me.

Daksh did leave me, but still held my hand and said Tik you are really cute, hope you get your perfect match soon. And I am sure you won't regret falling in love then.

I was just lost at that moment but still I don't know what made me ask,

So is Dhanno your perfect match Daksh?? Do you still feel she deserves you?

I don't know (saying this he took his usual long pause)

Then, Arey let's rush we still need to give the final touchup to the decor and then we can talk all night…

(I knew he just ignored my question, I knew he will never answer this question of mine)

I felt stupid at that time, wondering why I asked such a question. Was I expecting something from Daksh? Why am I feeling this strange closeness towards him? We just met few hours back and he was an all-time committed guy and I am gladly aware of that then why?

I think I should go home; it's quite late and moreover need to get up and rush for office tomorrow morning.

Hey I can drop you Tik … Please it's not safe for you to take a ride home at this hour and all the drop services from the office have left for tonight.

Seriously I wanted to spend some more minutes with him as tomorrow he will be back to his forced relationship with Dhanno. (I felt it was a pure nonsense relationship, and they did make a pathetic couple.)

On my way home, I looked at the moon that night and a thought just popped into my mind. "Just like the moon our heart becomes speechless sometimes, but as the moon feels the beauty of the night within itself and still stays calm, often our heart feels the beauty of some unforgettable moments but still stays calm."

Bye Daksh…Take care.

It was a fun filled night Tik, you are a great friend. Take care dear and don't forget me the moment I vanish from here today, do recognize me sometimes (winking at me).

When he left, suddenly my eyes had become wet, I was crying as if I lost my newly found love for the first time in my life. I immediately took a shower and was heading to sleep as I wanted to wipe off everything from my mind as soon as I woke up tomorrow.

Just then my phone had a message alert which read …

"Tonight when I hugged you, I seriously wanted to continue it till my last breathe. But sometimes life doesn›t allow reverting back your decision… I lived my entire life today with you and always will cherish this day with no regrets - Daksh…:)"

I smiled …

"A Speechless Moment where we both let our hearts become as speechless as the moon…"

Story narrated and thought by -

Pratiksha Misra

Conversations: Misunderstood

"Sometimes you fail by getting misunderstood and sometimes not understood at all"

"I heard she liked me even though I didn't,
Now she doesn't
even though I do.."

Why did you leave?

Why did you lie?

Why didn't you try?

Why didn't I think of leaving

Before you did?

Why didn't you respond with a clearer message?

Why are some questions

Just not answered?

Why did it get so dark?

Why did I think this to be magic?

When all of this is a tragical spark that refuses to end..

While I sit pretending this has no effect on me..

Conversations: With Love

"The kiss that made me wet
Lasted till sunset
Then I had to miss
It as the moment had left
The soul forever"

Conversations: With You

Take me
With you
I can walk
Along even hike
Take me with you
I can talk
Whatever you like
Take me with you
For I don't believe in memories
Cause
I only make up stories
With happy endings

Conversations: In Love

The last time I fell in love
I said I won't anymore
As I was pretty sure I course corrected
Not to feel anything…
I thought the last time
Was said and done
Until the last time got overwritten
With the new last time
That felt right again…

In Love

I ran faster

Only to know

That in love

You blink

With one eye

While the second

One lies right

Back at you

In Love

He came closer

My heart beat got faster

Only to know

That in love

Images are magnified

While you

Are getting blinder

By the day..

Story: New Year's Eve

I rushed to the hallway where I could reach him faster as I wanted to let him know how I felt for him.

Look there he is…

Found him! !!.. with a bunch of strangers and a weird look on his face

asking me to shoo away …

as I was still very much there staring as they were heading my way …

Like usual they righteously ignored my existence..

Still I stood there all by myself in the midst of a cheering crowd. (The New Year's Eve Party)

As the music got louder, felt annoyed by people's laughter, there shouts getting pitchy as it all grouped into a noisy bunch, pounding on my soul while my heart was sinking …

I tried real hard to keep up the false mask covering the face full of loathe.

Present Day ——-(After a Considerably Long Time)

Rushing to the door grabbing a toast, realized to have forgotten my glasses without which I become a next door neighbor to blindness.

Sometimes I believe every disability has to do something with your brain as it's definitely linked with what you think, you start believing it …as to what you really are..

Just last week had forgotten it twice but survived except few incidents here and there which followed in the chronological order:-

- Spilled ink all over Mr. Mathur's thesis.
- 10 heavy collisions with every single person who confronted me in the corridor including Mr. Mathur again.
- And just read "making out" loud in front of the class filled with 50 teenagers out of which one of them corrected me with a sheepish smile that the word was "melting out" which was written by none other than me in the black board just a few minutes back..

Gosh! !!, that makes me wonder..I am definitely Blind, there's no two ways about it..

Morning Rhea! !, greeted Mr. Mathur as I walked past him avoiding any sort of collision this time.

Statistics was my subject but when Elsa (my soul mate) was unavailable I ended up teaching English Literature to her students and hated it as they were full of romance, tragedy which were again filled with soliloquy, dramatic monologue.

Elegy -that depicts sorrow and lamentation when someone dies…

Don't we already do it when someone passes away… why to write it all…

The stuff had long before left my abode and had piled deep beneath numbers which for me was a lot simpler..

Hey is Elsa in today?

I inquired with Rakesh, our helper at the staffroom feeling a bit worried as she did have 3 drinks outside her limit at the theatre night yesterday….

Nahi Madam (No Madam), he replied with a smile and handed me a cup of tea comforting me as he knew I hated to take her classes when she was out…

Here I go again the very first class of my day was Hamlet and his remorseful saga to a class of 10 year olds, how interesting the day can be..

As I started off, there were those 2 twinkling eyes that followed me as I tried hard to explain them why Hamlet was unhappy with his mother. .somehow those eyes and the smile had the charm which I had felt a longtime back when I was young and pretty…It was disturbing but I went ahead with the lesson and got over with the class as soon as possible and rushed outside, when suddenly a hand reached out to me and a soft voice murmured ….

"Miss Can I Skip Hamlet and Go Directly to The Midsummer Night's dream?

To which I chuckled and looked back to find the same eyes gazing at me waiting for a reply..

I am sure you can my! , but what's wrong with Hamlet?

I don't like the way he talks to his mother.

The FlashBack..

Few Years Back —(Almost A Decade)

Rhea you need to come to me when you have any concern, I need to take care of you …

screaming loudly at me was my new boss Daksh, a smart handsome young man with a lot of arrogance.

And this was my 2nd week coping up with him as my boss, it was hard to adjust to the change plus he was good looking and I hated distractions at work.

Every single girl at work was talking about him..and was falling for him…

I was annoyed by the fact that he jumped in from nowhere to become my boss just because his father was the AVP of our multinational firm..How Convenient ….Grrrr…

I and my team had slogged day and night only to find that one day all the hard work gets banished in the black smoke of power and authority.

He was not unaware of his reputation especially among our team members and that was the reason why he pretended to be super nice with all of us..

Few months later we had become a close knit high performing team working together.All relationships in the world takes time to blend in and so did we…

I had my share of endless arguments with him in every single meeting,

we never agreed to each other no matter what but as soon as we walked out of the room,

every expression would be back in place in no time and people used to wonder if we were just fooling with each other back in the conference room..

We had started to look beyond professionalism, and had started to enjoy each other's company..

Most of the time I entered the team room looking out for him

His arrival added a ritual to halt at my desk while going ahead with his day..

Life has its own strange way of depicting relationships, most of us feel the same way that if 2 people from opposite sex spent more than normal time together they tend to either fall in love or have sex..

which I don't completely disagree but there is a 50% probability that they might be entirely having a different connection at a whole different tangent which not many realize can exist in every possible way..

Whenever I was stressed or upset, he used to pull me in for shopping, movie or a loud discussion in the terrace about love,sex,food,movie,how to date women at work pretty much every possible topic which had multiple facets associated with it..

Outside work, we never felt the urge to get together as we were completely packed up with our own sect of friends and family..

But we did text each other every time we felt the need to share something stupid or really close to heart..

By this time he had dated almost every decent to naughty chick at work.

There used to be special workshop sessions and meetings booked in one of our team conference rooms usually on Friday's and Saturday's on which I dreaded to be part of..

It would have an abrupt start with a most predicting end..where I am walking out of the room without taking down the next steps..

There was absolutely no romantic inclination from either one of us..just the fact that we had become each other's essential part of life in no time but had our own secrets to deal with as we came from disparate worlds.

Although one fine evening at a New Year Party where 80% alcohol was gushing through my blood, I

wanted to rush and tell him that he was really special for me.

When I realized the next day wanted to kill myself as I was kind of ruining it when there was a high probability of heart break.

Not sure why I had included myself among the people who either judged or misjudged a relationship by not thinking straight that there can be a truth of just simple liking and a strong bond where you care for the person and believe that he will stand for you whenever you need him…

Love is a dependency but friendship is the pure blend of affection and trust where you can expect to be betrayed by everyone except your one friend who will tug you in and be right beside you ready to fight all the battles of life..

Eventually this bonding came to an end with I quitting the organization for higher studies..

At first it was difficult to manage without each other.. but after a couple of years we got used to it..

And Love It Is ....

Thanks Ree! !, for taking care of my class yesterday..

Don't mention, hey wanted to know about a kid from the same class. His face looked familiar.

Naah! !!..too young 10 is not an eligible year to date.

Else, I was afraid if they all end up calling me granny..

Come on you are just 32, still very young just desperate and winked at me.

The next day I caught his watery eyes standing under the staircase on my way to the library.

Couldn't help moving towards him and hugging him tightly, comforting him …

what's the matter?

I miss being normal..

Walked along with him to his class room without anymore questions.

He was tormenting for some reason and it was none of my concern to know why but someone was pushing me inside to go for it and have all my answers.

The next day I was right outside his door and reaching out to his doorbell, to which an old lady answered. .

Is Vansh home, I am her teacher. .or his parents home?

Vansh So Raha Hai …(He is sleeping) and then she analyzed me for an entire 5 minutes after which she said

Kya Hua, Main Uski Daadi Hoon..(What happened, I am his granny you can tell me)

What about his parents? (I was poking this lady really bad, just waiting for her to slam the door on my face)

Instead, she invited me in and requested me to wait till Vansh gets up.

Dono mein jhagda hua aur ek din sab khatam, Vansh tab se yaheen hai mere paas…(Their parents are now separated and Vansh stays with her since he was a toddler)

Rhea Miss! !! I saw his face brightening up with an amazing fire.

His Granny smiled and rushed to the kitchen and got me some home made Theplas (A Dry Spicy Bread) and a cup of tea.

The warmth of the moment just dragged me into it forcing 5 hours of unlimited fun with the little one.

Harry Potter and his Chamber of Secrets while he passed out in deep slumber within 15 minutes,

his head resting on my lap as if he had waited a long time for this

My hands were on his forehead caressing him when suddenly felt a drop of water on his cheeks.

That was me …

Sometimes you take a decade to realize how much you are in love while at other times it takes just a couple of moments to feel the depth of an unspoken love..

Just yesterday I met this kid …

Wandering why I feel a heavy force tying me to this innocent plea for love.

SPLIT WIDE OPEN………………………………………………

Have You Lost It! !!

I can feel the agitation in her voice.

The last time I fell in love and right about the same time I felt God played some kind of prank on me

by making the person leave the world when there was just a month left before tying the knot..

She looked at me with painful eyes..

Don't do this to me again, I lost my child in front of my own eyes it would have been very much a part of me by now if only I was happily married with a fatherly figure to legally give birth to my own child..

What Crap …A girl is always pushed to the limit and a guy just gets a life full of options..

I am sure if I were dead instead f him, it wouldn't have been that big of a deal..

Relax Rhea..

I don't want to loose the second chance which God is giving me this time.Practically this child has no one except his granny, his parents are busy in their own world.Why should I be the one backing out.

When I am the one trying to become the fairy God Mother, because trust me this kid needs love and affection from a person who is selflessly happy of his existence.

Suddenly my eyes caught a text on my phone which said,

"You owe me an apologetic call as without father's permission one doesn't dare to mess with my child - Vansh's Dad"

And here comes the father ...Looking at Elsa I burst into laughter..

How is that funny? ?

I refrained myself from visiting Vansh anymore. Unfortunately he was always in my mind.

I tried to indulge into activities which would keep me busy all through the day and through the nights..

Took up evening mathematic classes for engineering graduates,started working out even though

used to stuff chocolates,ice creams watching Sholay, Pyaasa, Aradhana, Amar Prem (Bollywood Cult Movies)

I was wide awake through nights and was dozing off through days. .

You need to take a break Ree..

So you heard I slept at my desk when the final board exams were going on...

Think about your future, this is not what you want to become..

I want to be a successful mom,

Go ahead date guys marry someone successful and have tons of kids..

From my dreary eyes I could see Vansh staring at me from a distant at the corridor..

Is that Vansh?

How are you?, it seems my dad doesn't like meeting up with you but when will the day come when it will be about me..

I am sorry but hey guess what you can still talk to me whenever you want..

The same helplessness I felt sitting on the chair at the hospital with the doctor giving me a weird look..

So you are not married but you are pregnant and where is this guy??

He is dead can we go ahead with the process please..

It's Not The End ....

Life had taken a weird turn as suddenly the path on which I went ahead long time back seem to be stalking me back leaving me no choice …

Couldn't get past the loss that I had no more chances.

While walking back to the staff room saw a figure standing right next to the door separating the staff room and the guest room..My eyes were playing games as they were too damp to even read through glasses but still trying to focus the figure as it looked familiar.

As my vision got closer couldn't refrain my heart pounding hard realizing the figurine to be none other than the one back from the new year's eve..

He tilted his head grinning back at me as his face glowed "Is That You Rhea? ..

Within couple of seconds my head was on his shoulders with uncontrollable tears rolling down my eyes.I could hear his heart pounding as well as this time his grasp was tighter than usual.There was a moment of absolute silence and I could smell his Davidoff which had haunted me for days after that dreadful New Year's Eve.

Never felt it was you Rhea …all this while with Vansh.

Wiping my face, I stood there looking at him - I still feel he needs me at the moment but I will leave it up-to you to decide …

You tell me what went wrong?

Frankly, I don't know much just that his eyes say it all and to me it's overwhelming that he has chosen me ..

I love him too..believe me. .

Where were you? ..

He held my hands and coming closer looked straight into my eyes.

I was there but I would not lie was busy figuring out some other stuff in my life but would have come back to him eventually..

When?…(This time my eyes were sternly looking at him as if trying to ask him millions of questions since the New Year's Eve)

Don't bother to answer …I am happy that you still care have my class to go to.

Walking down the corridor my heart got heavier as if I lost everything back again and this time I drowned too deep to even have the courage to fight back the waves and swim to the coast as I loved the way I was sinking..

After school I went to the roof top where we used to chat for hours (I and Daksh).

It was an amazing sight from above as you can feel the whole city but not the noise and dust, you can reach out to the stars but can never touch them, you will always find the person within the organization you are searching for if you stand there for an hour and you can always stand over the edge hoping that you will never fall as there will be always someone accompanying you who will never leave you when you tend to fall..

Our organization had moved to their new building, no one was there except me..staring at those times which had no wings to fly back..

Found You! !

Hey! !, what you doing here?

I came to apologize for always closing doors on you and now taking away all your hopes for me.

——- After A Year

Aresto Momentum! !! (A Harry Potter Spell to decrease velocity)…as I drove past the traffic lights just in time.

Hope we are gonna make it to the exhibition..

Elsa! !! Did I miss it …

Let's walk in ...

For the first time ever it felt a bit awkward to be honest but was socializing with all the parents in a different way and rushed to the "Metal Detector" counter.

How's it going buddy?

Relax, all said and done we will nail it ...

As the tall lady (Judge) was approaching us and she exclaimed " He Looks very much like you Rhea ...

I Was Speechless as we both smiled and winked at each other.(Both -Vansh & Me)

Staring straight at the auditorium door each time trying hard to see the figure which had held me to not let me go for the first time ever in my lifetime.

Just when someone tapped on my head as hard to get my attention. .

Grabbing my hand and pulling it over. .This time let's spend the New Year's Together..(It Was Daksh)

.... *Story narrated and thought by: -*

Pratiksha Misra

Conversations: Reasons I Like You

For all the reasons
That I like you
Are the very same reasons
For which I don't like myself

For the same reasons
I can see
You are clearly free
While I still
Fly alone
Tying myself
Into a naked branch
All day long thinking
About things that went wrong

For those reasons
Are unfair
But from far
It seems

Those reasons
Have cast such a shadow
Upon you
That makes you
Very much unlike you
And I wish
Someday it will turn me
Somewhat like you
If I stay longer with you…

Conversation: Conversation Starter

Do you look for me
In the dark?
No, I look for you
In every spark..

Do you look for me
Only when no one's around?
No, I hear you
Even when there's no sound..

Do you look for me
Even now?
No, I fear if I do
I will lose you somehow..

Do you think
About how I used to look?
No, I remember
The day you returned the book
While I took your pen
Only to start a conversation then..

"Love doesn't stand by itself"

"You don't die to fulfill other's wishes; you die because you are done washing other people's used dishes"

Conversations: People

"We almost arrive
And are ready to leave
But what if you can't leave
Even if you wanted
That's when you start
Exploring the place and people
Which you didn't begin
Doing in the first place"

Empty Seats
Empty Streets
Empty treats
Empty feet

Empty Pockets
Empty Sockets
Empty Baskets
Empty Pallets

Empty Skies
Empty Cries
Empty tries
Empty Denies

"The unknows places
& awkward smiles
To empty seats
& inward miles
Pieces of the same puzzle
Put together
In different order.."

"The people who look
Outside from their window
Are always different
Than the ones
Not peeping through
Their windows at all.."

Story: Coincidence

The fog thickened, obscuring the road and making driving treacherous. The wind howled, rattling the windows. Suddenly, my car stalled, refusing to climb the hill. Water surged down, shaking the vehicle as I sat inside, my legs trembling.

I abandoned the car and decided to walk, joining the chaotic mass of people scrambling for safety. The wet, crowded path was a free-for-all, with everyone prioritizing their own survival. I was shoved, nearly falling into the filthy water, when a hand gripped mine and pulled me into a thatched shop. Water dripped from the roof, but it felt safer than the dangerous rush outside.

The eyes beneath the black hood looked familiar. Initially blurry, they sharpened into focus, and I recognized them instantly.

"How have you been?" he whispered. "Stay right here. Don't move. Trust me."

He pulled me close, sheltering me as the crowd surged. People clung to each other, desperately trying to escape the floodwaters that swept down the hill, carrying away anyone who lost their footing. I could hear his heart beating again. Tears streamed down my face as I realized how much time had passed. I had fallen asleep that night hoping to hear from him, but all I'd found was a noisy silence.

I couldn't complain. I snuggled closer, resting my head on his shoulder. People screamed, fights erupted, babies cried, but I was calm, closing my eyes and sleeping as if I hadn't slept in a decade. He stood like a pillar while others pushed and shoved, trying to escape the flood.

Suddenly, he shook my shoulder. "Time to wake up."

I opened my eyes. It was almost dusk. The rain, which had started flooding the streets that morning, had subsided, and the water level had dropped. People were returning to their homes before the next downpour. It was still light enough to see, and I tried to discern the face behind the familiar eyes. I knew who it was, but I was afraid to ask. If it had all been a dream, I wasn't ready to wake up.

"I should get going, Tiksha. Stay safe!" he said, disappearing into the crowd. I watched him leave, rooted to the spot, awakening from my deep sleep with my name echoing in my ears, just the way I loved to hear it.

Smiling to myself, I ordered a cutting chai at a roadside shop, looked up, trying to find the moon behind the clouds, and murmured, "Why didn't I stop him? I could have asked him something."

His last words echoed in my mind: "Don't ever ask me to come back, because I will never be able to."

Driving home, a tear trickled down my cheek. I wiped it away, consoling myself with the thought that this chance encounter was a sign, a way to keep my love alive. Love finds its way, even when it's not easy.

Conversations: Love Me the Same

Will You Love Me The Same?

If I told you I am older

Will you love me the same way

If I told you I am a cold person

Will you love me the same way

If I told you all that I haven't told anyone yet

Will you love me the same way

If I told you I get depressed pretty often

Will you hold me the same way

If I told you I cannot impress anyone everyday

Will you spend time with me the same way

If I told you I can be pretty challenging

If I told you I am aging and there are wrinkles under my skin that I hide with makeup

If I told you I am not adjusting and don't talk to

anyone if I don't have to

If I told you I don't dress up on days and eat cereals from the box in a messy way

Will you be with me the same way

Are you still listening or you have run away

If I told you I don't forget easy

And can stalk you for days making you feel uneasy

If I told you I can be dangerously hunting insects

And can jump in muddy water for hours

If I told you I am not afraid of blood

And I can fight until I hear the sound go thud

Will you still sit with me watching sunset in the park

Hold hands while mosquitoes fly around and overlook the dark

If I told you I don't cry

I keep trying not to but if I do I do end up lying that I am not

If I told you I don't have a lot of friends but when pushed to a crowd I pretend I am having fun

If I told you dark stories of memories that I have lived

Will you still respect that my feelings can be genuine

If I told you I can stick to a cave and have conversations by the grave

Will you be bothered by my interests and just leave the premises

If I told you that I don't want to be seen

If I told you that life is pretty when you are hidden

Will you still come hide with me or want me to make a continuous effort to blend in

If I told you, looks like you are gone

I didn't plan on telling you everything that I just admitted

But looks like you just made up your mind, blindly as you just want things to be repeated

Even though it's a circle of being cheated by the one

you promise to love their inner most

Conversations: That's What I am Thinking

Water drops
Keeps dripping fom the tap at night
While noone will try to close
As it starts dampening floors
Atleast that's what I am thinking
Will end up happening…

Blood drops
From my finger that got slaughtered
By a kitchen knife
While there's noone around
Or atleast not to be found
Who can come running
As it starts pouring on the pretty dress
That I am wearing for the evening..
Atleast that's what I am thinking
Will end up happening…

Amidst the firmament
You couldn't help a sudden fall
Bruising your knee as they
Start making the thinnest crossword puzzle
While blood oozes out from each block
As it trickles down tearing the tinseltown
Atleast that's what I am thinking
Will end up happening..

Story: The Guilt Trip

September 25, 2016

The Guilt Trip

A usual weekday tired of the heat and hard work at the hospital.The hot day had made me weary already as I was tempted to sit down and doze off every few minutes before my shift's end until some one feels the urge to wake me up from my deep slumber.But that couldn't happen as I was tending back to back patients needing immediate assistance.

Finally returning from my shift caught the last train but my place wasn't coming up sooner until it stops at approximately 20 stations in between.Grabbed a cozy corner where I could execute my earlier plan with minimum botheration.

"Did I wake you up? "..said a familiar voice which I was not hoping to hear ever again in my lifetime.

A familiar instinct poked me that this is got to be some dream where I am traveling different worlds as the person who was asking me the question was hidden in a chamber inside the casket full of memories which had made all attempts to get faded a long time back.

"How are you? " as he smiled with those magical eyes, his face had started to get blurry through my watery vision.I was fumbling failing to make sense at the same time while my feet kept shaking with trembling shoes making me trip everywhere as I tried to get a stronger grip of me so that I can forcibly get a chance to wake up pulling myself back to reality.

Right when those hands had pulled me tightly so I slowly stopped fighting myself.

Giving up finally by resting my heavy head down deeper listening to his heart beats.Closed my eyes calming down the rage inside, wondering if this moment had any possibility to exist in real.

"I missed you! ", I exclaimed an instant sigh came along with my tone getting heavier as I spoke.

Couldn't make out much from the other side either.

Moments of silence as the next stops got announced in order playing as a regular side track on my mind as I kept sleeping peacefully after decades of restlessness.

" I should get going but it was a miracle to see you in person", whispering those words into my ears moved my head from his lap where I was sleeping with my mouth wide open.

Adjusted my head on my laptop bag tending my messy hair from my forehead, kissing lightly on my cheeks.

Why didn't he make the slightest attempt to wake me up before leaving?

As I thought suddenly a jerk accompanied by a painful thud woke me up as I fell licking the cabin floor.Opened my eyes to the vicious truth grabbed my bag and walked out the door.

Tears rolled down making those eyes wet wiping off the kiss from those cheeks drying them back to senses as I had found myself exactly at the same spot when he walked away from my life leaving me all alone.

Rushing into the dark hallway searching for my room keys caught hold off his lighter in my bag instead still very much there which I used to offer when he pulled out a cigarette and kept digging into his pockets miserably staring at me smiling sheepishly for me to help him out without saying a word.

The days where we started off with heated arguments and the moment his eyes fell on a tiny scratch in my finger, it would unknowingly make him hold my hands and keep comforting gently ignoring every word I said after.

God! , where are my damn keys as a drop of blood trickled down with a pin piercing my finger.

"It doesn't matter anymore", speaking to the finger crazily took out my keys and went inside.

That should never happen again I kept grumbling with the mirror while brushing my teeth that night.

"Move On! - read it loud."

were the words my permanent marker had written on the whiteboard stuck to my refrigerator to which I glanced through taking the last gulp of juice.

I forced myself to read it as loud as possible crying out loud enough to help my heart recover from the earlier drench of the guilt trip which I have to get rid of sooner in order to move ahead ignoring the fact that the wound might have dried away after healing, but the scar still remains alive and prominent after 5 years from moaning his death.

Conversation: With Friends

How often do you feel like everyone is thinking something and talking something else?

How often do you avoid someone because they don't feel like the same anymore?

How often you have to keep saying nicer things otherwise you feel they will just hang up?

How often you feel people like the wrong you as you don't think they will end up liking the real you?

How often your child bursts into tears, and you stand there while making your mind that she needs to deal with this experience herself?

How often you walk backwards to settle your ego and apologize, but you simply cannot?

How often you have heard someone talking about you, when you get to overhear and you fear this is it?

How often when you voice your opinions that isn't in sync with what the person in front of you has bought you a drink for?

"There is always a friend beside you..

but the one inside you needs to know that one is the right one for you.."

My grandfather once said, "a friend can be highly annoying to every other one in the room, but will always be different the moment you walk up next to her/it/they/him."

My elder brother was my first logical friend, since a kid who guided me, about the essence of friendship, of what we look in a friend? and used to factor me into his friendly mix, early on to give me an experience of it beforehand. I call it experimenting the truth of life with someone or a group of people, who are highly likely to never hurt you whatsoever, as you are so timid in front of them, that they feel like protecting you.

I remember, he being up the whole night teaching me a break dance number on the song of famous Prabhu Deva, during sixth grade talent show, so that I get to climb the popularity ladder instead of crawling under the shelf of cobwebs. I finally did pass the test, and there was no looking back after. The thing with popularity is just don›t get too blindly into it, landing on the surface is just fine, while flying too high, might land you with broken bones, that I was definitely not a fan of.

Then came my parents my second friends, as I spent almost 22 years with them, in the same house and to be honest they are pretty brutal when it comes to active feedback on my social skills till date. My mom just couldn›t stop her from giving feedback about every friend who came around and she used to even predict the longevity of our friendship.

For those who haven't read the **first part** ,this is for you …

There are times, when a small girl wants to be desperately invited to a birthday, get to know the world that is outside of school, glamorous and gorgeous with games, candy, cakes, yummy delicacies, and friends in pretty dresses. Yes that was me, in 5th grade, trying to fit in and making sure I get invited to every birthday party I can make it to. I used to be very upset if I wasn't invited. That's the feeling of being left out.

That is a baggage that you carry everywhere you go, to get invited, to get considered, to get smiled at, to get to belong and fit into a place as quickly as possible.

I had a tough time fitting into college as a day scholar at first (a person who doesn't get a dorm room, and stays with either a local guardian or parents). The 12th results were out, and as usual I didn't fair well as expected, with results comes the awkwardness of friends who have certainly scored well, forming a sort of alliance, where obviously if your scores are lower, you go invisible at a span of cease to exist anymore. Specially with the girl clan, it's either you have to be rich or you need to have an extraordinary score card, or you need to like the same boy. Which in my case none of them held priority in the same order.

But with time, friendship is all about getting to work with what you have versus rooting for someone who physically doesn't exist. I started to get along with the folks who were readily available, in the parking garage, in the mechanical lab, in the middle of a lecture, and an exciting journey of eternal bonding started with just few fart jokes, and common grounds of being a middle class philosopher trying to pursue a career in computer science engineering. Gender wasn't an issue this time, as all types of genders are permitted in grad colleges.

There is a phase of epic loss in friendship, during college time, as because we tend to talk to anyone and everyone. There is clearly a percentage of crowd, that gets calculated in a diminishing factor. Like the lab results are always on the basis of approximation of a zero error, similarly your friends are always on the approximation of mostly erroneous encounter than finding an actual character that will bond forever. And thereby by the time you manage to get your first paycheck in your first ever legit job, these friends are nowhere to be found.

Then there is a feeling of belong, that I brought up earlier. During 5th grade, of my Carmel Convent School, there was a huge group, that everyone wanted to be a part of, I even attended an interview panel to get through this group. But by the time I qualified, something inside me convinced myself, to get out of it and have a group of likeable lot rather than be judged a lot, that triggered a court room for classroom drama.

By college, you kind of know that these groups, are just vicious torture circles, where though you have a sense of belonging, but even if one fine day you don't show up, they will still distribute the pack of cards and start playing without you.

That's when you start looking for those eyes, that seek you, those one off folks who stand next to you, when everyone else has butchered your existence. I had a college incident, where I was returning from a tiring workshop and got bullied by a bunch of seniors, I shouted and fought back, only to my surprise that the next day my whole batch, had been asked not to talk to me. That's when some of the handful lot, stood beside me as they mocked at the ridiculous misdirected rule passed by a bunch of bullies.

Those were the friends not a group as not one person knew another, but they knew the real me, and still didn't thought of running away. For the second time I felt good, the first time was when I had friends rooting for me at a dare, where I sang a funny song about a guy who was too shy to be true.

"Friends need to know, what it is that you bring to the table, rather than just forcing you to eat left overs."

Addiction of friends, realism, sense of belonging, sense of frequent responses, sense of indifferences, never goes away, no matter where you are at your life. Even with wrinkles, you need that one friend, who you wink at and they understand what you mean. With friends you feel that sense of fulfillment, of heading somewhere, no one has ever taken you before. Where even at the middle of night, you can fight and make up, at the same time. With whom getting a scoop of chocolate ice cream and a bike ride while singing Kishore Kumar and Rafi's songs are eternal bliss.

The worst part of friendship is when a friend asks you, why are you mean to her friend?, when all this while you ended up waiting for her in the rain by the bus stop. You are so confident, that your friend is just yours forever, until that bubble gets busted and there is someone else who is far more important for them.

There is this constant poking inside, that you want to hide, as that friend becomes someone else's friend in no time and the seat beside you has gotten empty again. For me departure of friends, was heartbreaking, as finding a friend again from scratch for a person like me, was hard, because I don't forget like a spell of never happened.

What's the philosophy of seeking someone else other than the one you have?

Why isn't that someone who literally left a warm meal to shiver right next to you not enough?

Why do we pretend we have a lot going while no one else is waiting back at home?

I had friends in a scattered manner, during college, and I literally used to spend hours talking to them on phone, driving my two wheeler to their houses, making acquaintances with their siblings, trying to solve their boyfriend problems, trying to solve their career dilemma, while all this while there was no one for me. And I had made up my mind, after some pretty flawed solutions I was groped up into, which were far more messy, than getting stuck in your own grave at one point, harder to die, harder to try. I finally pledged to start handling myself with much sophistication and entourage by the help of my first ever furry friend, **Tiny** and my journal, writing everyday.

I remember I was slapped once on my cheeks at high school, by a girl, who I hardly was familiar with, but the part that was more painful, that all the spectators surrounding me when that incident occurred, right in front of them, were supposed to be my friends but no one did anything heroic to save me from this hideous lady who thought it was okay to physically abuse a person out in public. I didn't react at all, I took that slap as an act of learning, that I wasted my time with the people, who were never meant to be by my side.

While I was in Mumbai to search for a job from scratch, I knew no one, not even my room mate, she was a kind soul, but still, day one, started from not knowing her at all to the day she gave me courage to not give up on my quest of finding a job by actually pivoting my journey to give startups a chance.

After which, I had started to make friends with shopkeepers, gatekeepers, a man who irons clothes for a living, a girl who sells mobile phone sim cards, a transgender lady who blesses me every time I rushed to catch the train giving her a ten rupee note, an auto rickshaw driver, who taught me the art of saving money using public transportation, a cobbler who fixed the hole in my shoe, right before an interview for free. There was a never ending trail of remarkable friendships.

You need to be a friend that makes living easier as it goes a long way. Being an outsider, in my starting days in Mumbai, I had learned to be part of multiple groups, be friends with strangers, go back to friends from my childhood and college that never got over me, and find friends that always found me no matter what.

At that time I did make friends at work, but they always made me alienated after a while. As they zoned out at the fact, of me entering their world from a comparatively lesser outlook than they had about movies, music, entertaining gimmicks, places of fun, multitude of people knowing them from forever and so on and so forth. Even got cheated on with stealing, betrayal once or twice, which pushed me into the darker caves of solitude, where I was too scared to mingle with anyone anymore.

The addiction of a person who likes similar things is hard. It's like the drug, you feel like having on days you feel the worst. A call, a message, a known face, a familiar tone, a sensation that you still mean something, a conversation that fills the room with emotions and a notion, that you are amiable and worth a shot.

If you call me a friend,
I promise not to pretend,
But if I am not,
following till the end,
then this might be a twisted bend,
that got entangled,
to an illusive knot..

A friend is someone,
who brings that laugh,
when you had it rough,
until someone asks,
that you had enough,
while you leave the store,
there's a smoke and a choke,
with the echo of giggling encore,
right after..

It's when you sit with them..
you know them,
it's when you talk to them..
you know them,
it's when you walk with them..
you know them,

it's when you are alone with them..
you know them,
you don't make friends amidst crowds with
noises..
you make friends hidden in smiley corners, or teary eyes,
where secrecy lies, or an exclusive call to your inner sighs..
Or where time flies, while you are the same girl sitting
alongside a plate that just got filled with the most cheesy fries..

"It is the hellos

& goodbyes

that make up

the world

worth living in…"

Until next time, keep up with the conversations….

About the Author Pratiksha Misra

An artist by heart, writing passionately since a long time about my experiences with life so far. A working mom, an animal lover, a runner, and a woman of color trying to make her voice heard in a society that's slowly changing for good.

I was Born and raised in Rourkela, Odisha, India, and now settled for a living with my husband and daughter, in Media, Pennsylvania, USA. Numerous thoughts published for free in my blogs like JustUtter, Speechless Moon and Innocent Thoughts.

Books by This Author

Bhoota Gappa: 7 Short Horror Stories by JustUtter (JustUtter Horror) "Bhoota Gappa", means "Ghost Stories", in Odia, and that's my native language from the land of Jagannath, where I come from called Odisha. This all started back in 1985, when we used to visit Buxi bazar, Cuttack, our grandparents house during summer holidays. As stories were a kid's portal to imagination back then, we were narrated an infinite number of stories, by my grandmother (father's mom), most of it in the genre of ghosts, spirits, black magic, which either she had experiences of her own or she narrated experiences of someone close to her from her childhood.

She called it "Bhoota Gappa". I name this book series in memory of my grandmother, who wanted to become a great educator some day and read a lot of books in various languages, despite of being educated just till middle school.

Each book in this series, consists of 7 short horror stories, followed by a snippet of a bigger horror story happening in parallel, with all the characters from these shorter stories. Some of these experiences are being shared for the first time and are stories inspired by an amalgamation of true stories and events. This will make your heart beats faster, your eyes get bigger and your minds a bit foggy, while you feel chillier as you walk deeper into the darkness of these haunting experiences. Hope you read it all and publish some honest feedback after you read. Innocent Thoughts - Part 2: A Real Journey Build Just with Thoughts Come follow me in this journey of innocent thoughts, where you fall in love, but you still can't help heartbreaks, where you tie yourself in numerous relationships, filled with grief, loss and happiness. Where success can be defined by failure. Don't judge this world where joy of inheritance exists alongside pretences, where seasons come and go, but emotions can't resist your inner child, which no matter how wild they get, remain untouched. Innocent Thoughts: A Book of Experiences & Poetry Innocent thoughts started in the year 2009. It's a collection of poems, stories, experiences, and much more. Some pieces sound like being written by a little girl and yes they very much are, as back when I started to write these pieces in my journal I had just begun middle school. It all started when there was a writing event in the 5th grade and our class teacher late Miss Udita had given an exciting introduction. There were 2 portions of the event one was to write a poem starting with "I wish…" and the second was a story "It was a night filled with chilled darkness…". I bagged the third position for my story and got a round of appreciation for my poem as well.

I kept writing after that as regularly as possible while it made me grow fonder to the life I was living in and also a way to question my actions when I penned it down. It has helped me grow in phases and still aids me to give a soothing touch for my readers in the words where I express that we all are drifting in the same boat called life. In a phase of me when trying to forget a lot of people that left me with their sudden demise, this was a way where I could talk to them and tell them how much I missed them, but knowing that there is no way I could ever reach out to them again and have a conversation.

In a phase of me when revisiting and discovering myself when I quit my job in Mumbai, I started to realize there are experiences which you cannot avoid. Friends holding your back, Family accepting you whenever possible, losses, happiness, betrayal and then one night I finally gave in to the thought of opening a blog filled with my writings as a portal of me conversing and giving my learned lessons to the world in the form of "Innocent Thoughts". In a phase of me when I fell in love, dealing with heartbreak and connecting with the ones who are there around me for good. Experiencing lament, grief, nuance, repeating mistakes, undertaking a hollowness then filling it up all over again.

In a phase of me becoming a mother and sharing motherhood with all the new mothers around and redefining the meaning of love and the sensible feeling of responsibility when you are so new to all of it. Now I am enjoying being a mother of my 5-year-old and pretty much confided in a world of my own but sometimes I feel we all grow at our own separate pace with experiences refining the virtuous ladder as we move along. So until these experiences keep teaching me to be fair and square I would be writing my thoughts and looking out for similar thoughts from your end.

Don't hesitate to reach out to me anytime with your suggestions. There are many other related works which you can check as Speechless Moon, Just Utter. Please feel free to reach out and connect with me.

"It takes great courage to say you can write, even more, to write exactly how you feel"

www.ingramcontent.com/pod-product-compliance
Lightning Source LLC
LaVergne TN
LVHW041118150826
845673LV00007B/2106

9798897249978